THE MAGIC QUILT

BY BLAIR THOMPSON ILLUSTRATED BY FRED WILLINGHAM

SUNDANCE PUBLISHING

Ms. J. Delucchi

Text *The Magic Quilt* © 1995 by Blair Thompson
Illustrations © 1995 by Fred Willingham

Published by Sundance Publishing
234 Taylor Street, Littleton, MA 01460

ISBN 1-56801-786-3
10 9 8 7 6 5 4 3 2 SP

I cannot sleep at night,
I sit and wait for the light.

Mom is very far away,
And I miss her every day.

But Gram tells me she knows what is troubling my head
And how she will keep me safe and snug in my bed.

In the morning when I wake, we'll make a magic quilt —
The safest, warmest comforter that ever was built.

A special quilt made from Mom's clothes
That will keep me warm and safe, letting me doze.

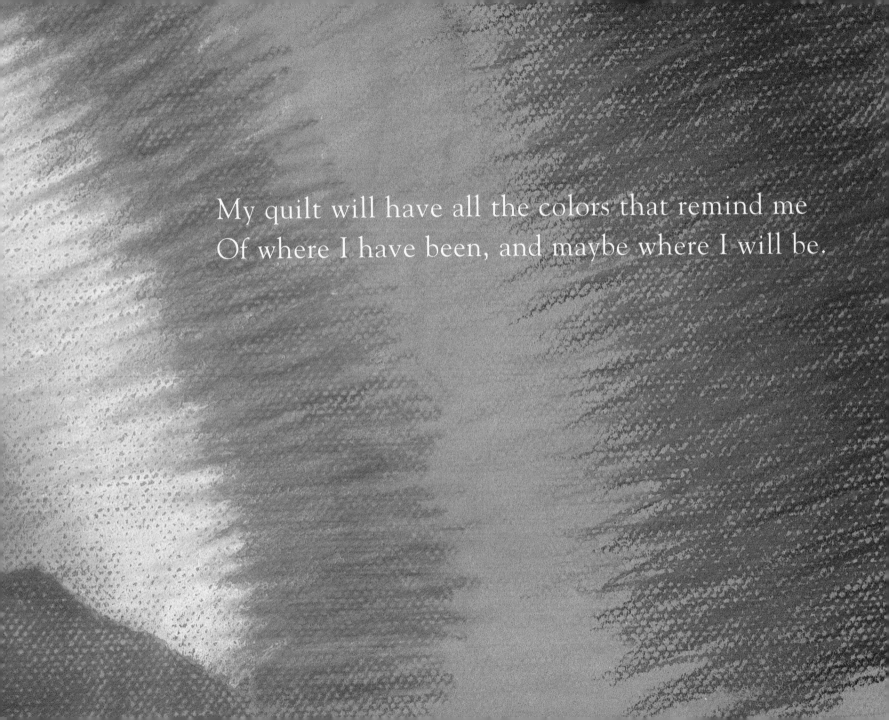

My quilt will have all the colors that remind me
Of where I have been, and maybe where I will be.

With circles of yellow and glittering gold,
Round and jolly like the sun, and warm I'm told.

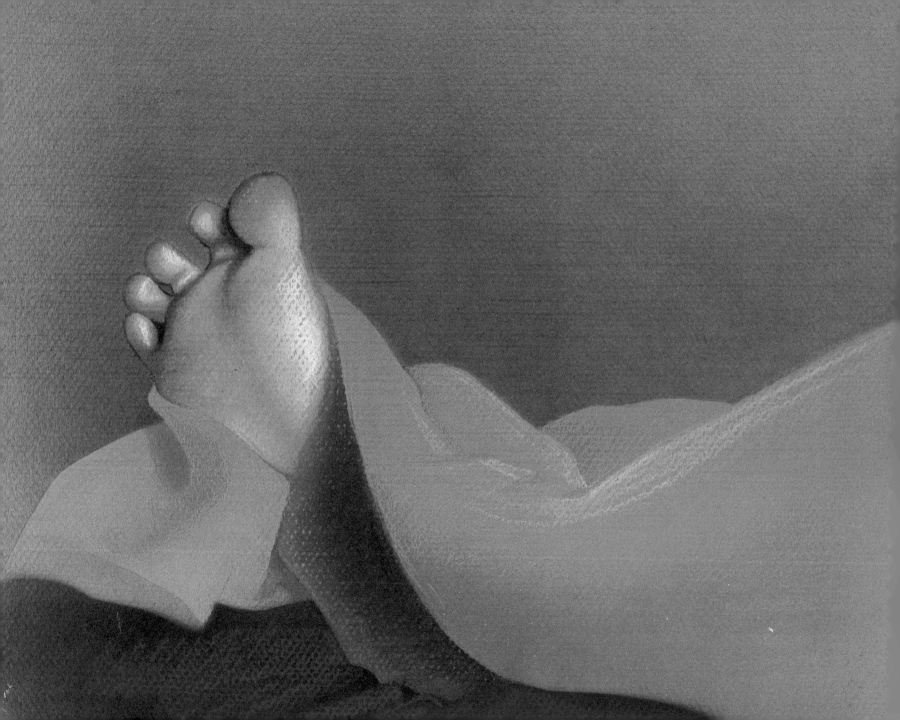

And patches of pink silky soft like a rose,
To tickle my tummy and my ten brown toes.

Orange shapes like a fall pumpkin or an autumn leaf,
Thick and fluffy to encircle me like a reef.

Deep green forests that are tall enough to hide
My many, many dreams that will grow inside.

And some royal purple fit for a queen.
To hold me tightly while I wish and dream.

Gram and me, we will cut and we'll sew
Creating a magic quilt to show.

And then late at night when it's just me,
Why I'll laugh and giggle, feeling free.

Sad and afraid, I will no longer be.
Instead I'll be wrapped in Mom's memory.

Then I can dream of what was and will be
And Mom will be there, on the bed with me.